Consumed by the Professor

DEANN SOLEIL

Professor Mariah White has finally secured the career of her dreams she had been chasing for years as a college professor. When Cyrus crosses her path during her dirty 30 birthday night out then appears on her class roster, everything changes.

He knows something damaging about her past that can ruin her, causing him to hold it against her. To not lose the career she has wanted forever, she must play his game and comply every step of the way.

Does she give in to Cyrus's demands, or does she deal with the repercussions that can come from her secret being released?

Content Warnings

Consumed is a quick forbidden romance; however, some topics can be difficult to read.

Some topics that can be found within this book are:

- Infidelity
- Drug Use (Cocaine)
- Blackmail
- Professor/Student
- Reverse Age Gap
- Instalove (From MMC)
- Enemies to Lovers
- Forced Proximity
- Unrequited Love
- Divorced FMC
- Obsessed MMC
- Alcohol Consumption
- Sexual Choking

For those who felt a quiet pull for the professor they could never have.

Spice Checklist

Will she give in to

yrus's demands?

SCHOOL OF
SOCIAL WO

Prologue: Mariah

SUMMER OF 2018

I always dreamed about what life would look like for me when I went to college. Starting the program, I was uncertain what to select for a major because I wasn't even fully confident in what I found joy in. But, as I entered my senior year of undergraduate school, I knew my decision to major in social work had been the right path for me.

I've always had a passion for helping those who are less fortunate and giving back to the community, and it got to the point that, when I was a little girl, people always asked me what I wanted to be when I grew up. For the longest time, I told everyone I desired to be a teacher, but I knew with just an undergraduate degree, that wasn't plausible. Knowing that, I planned to go back to school to get my master's and reach that goal. My confidence in my communication skills and desire to help others succeed pushed me toward pursuing that, so I could become a successful college professor.

While at Redon University, I wasn't looking to settle down; I just wanted to focus on my studies. At least, that is what I'd convinced myself. That was until I met Billy during my freshman year in one of my classes. With his brown hair, hazel eyes, and six-foot stature, he was the furthest thing from an eyesore. And shockingly, because of the similarities we shared, the two of us clicked and fell in love. With our shared interests in volunteering and fishing, we connected on deeper levels that made falling for one another as easy as breathing.

It helped that he has supported my desire to graduate and become a professor from the very beginning. He always told me my personality emanated the aura of someone capable of changing the world, someone who others could turn to in a time of need.

Over the years, we had so much fun getting to know one another, and before our senior year, he asked if I'd be interested in joining him on a cruise to the Bahamas. With us having only been dating for a few years, it caught me off guard that he was so willing to pay for us to go on such an extravagant vacation, especially considering we were both broke college students.

On the last day of the cruise, we went up to the pool deck to watch the sunset, and before I knew it, he was down on one knee asking me to spend the rest of my life with him. It was the easiest yes I had ever uttered because of our compatibility and how much we'd grown together throughout the years. Calling him my fiancé after that brought me so much joy, making me eager to finish the school year so we could take the next step toward marriage.

When the summer ended and the preparations for school began, my outlook on life changed. I'd often catch myself sitting down to look at my ring, reflecting on the happiness the last four years had brought me and how grateful I was to have found my forever person. Imagining my life as anything other than what it'd become was impossible because I knew in the very marrow of my bones that I was on the right path toward a career I'd dreamed of pursuing and with someone who loved and supported me every step of the way.

With the semesters of senior year flying by, my mind fixated on how much closer I was to becoming a professor. Knowing that I was approaching a position where further education and experience were required, I'd reached the point where I needed to decide what to do next.

Finally settling on a decision, I applied to the Master of Social Work program at Redon University. I'd elected to go that route so I could stay connected to the faculty and staff that I developed relationships with and learned from over the past four years. And when I received my acceptance letter, I was beyond ecstatic to share the news with Billy and embark on a new educational journey.

With the beginning of the school year approaching, Billy and I discussed our desire to be married before I graduated from the two-year program. To ensure I could become Mrs. Harrington before graduation, we decided to get married on May 30, 2018. With our desire to save money, we went back and forth on the type of wedding we wanted, and ultimately, we opted for something small with our closest family and friends. Walking down the aisle to say 'I do' was a moment I could never compare to any other part of my life, and it made me excited for what would come next.

After the wedding, the pursuit for my degree started kicking my ass from time to time, and often left me questioning why I'd started in the first place.

Who would've known there was so much involved in becoming a social worker, and that practicums were required to gain experience? In my first year, I elected to do my practicum as a medical social worker in a children's emergency department. And boy, let me tell you how heartbreaking that was. Seeing children who had been victims of violence—with the youngest being a two-year-old—was something I never wished to see, but knowing how much I could help them became so rewarding.

This year, I am getting close to the end of my practicum in the school setting, where I've worked with students who were facing academic challenges. My experiences and joy working with them reassured me that teaching is most definitely my calling because of the love I have for witnessing the wide range of experiences students have. With everything I've learned alongside them, I've noticed that I can teach based on the foundations I have built and my combined experiences in the fields of medical and school-based social work.

Most people asked me why I went to school to be a social worker when teaching was my passion, and my answer to their question became simple: being a social worker meant I could get my license and provide therapy on the side when I wasn't teaching. One of the core values of social work is the desire to help others, and both jobs provided me the opportunity to do just that.

The journey to obtain my degree was worth it, and extremely rewarding. The satisfaction of all of my hard work truly paid off when graduation came, and Billy and my family showed up as my biggest supporters. When they called my name, every one of them stood up, whistling my name as I was handed my master's degree, and that moment continues to be one of the most surreal experiences I've ever had.

Having applied for a few jobs in the school setting to get my foot in the door before applying for a teaching position, I kept reminding myself that I deserved to follow my dreams. Fortunate enough to secure a position as the Student Support Coordinator at Redon University, I found myself in a role that would enable me to advance to a professorial position in a few years. It was a job I immediately fell in love with because it allowed me to interact with students, while also giving me the chance to expand my social work lens to help them overcome struggles they faced.

Through it all, my relationship with Billy had only grown. Recently, he brought up the topic of having children, and I expressed that I wasn't sure if that was something I was ready for yet. I didn't want to rush into having children and risk straining our relationship by adding that responsibility to the mix. And, in expressing that to him, we came to the consensus that perhaps one day we would, but until then, I would continue to love him as he loved me, and show up as the best version of myself at the job I'd come to adore.

SCHOOL O
SOCIAL WO

Mariah

The past few years brought both ups and downs. Being a Student Support Coordinator has allowed me to learn a great deal about the students at Redon University. On many occasions, they come into my office to talk about life and how challenging school is for them. Every conversation reminds me how much I truly enjoyed my job, and gives me a lot to look forward to each day.

My romantic life, on the other hand, has been something else. Billy and I started off really well—with the same common goals, wants, and needs—but over time, that stability dwindled. I never realized how much a relationship can change when you live with someone, constantly sharing space with them on a daily basis. It was definitely something I learned the hard way. One day, everything could go well, and then the next, my world would turn upside down.

At 29, I really thought my life would have excelled, but of course, it was the opposite. Billy and my relationship has become strained over the past five years due to complications and differences in opinions. With my dark past, and the regret I hold for things that cause some of my concerns, I have dragged Billy through hell over the last few years. It is something I am sorry for, but he is also a part of the problem. As they say, it takes two to make a relationship work, but I have not been happy for a while.

When I first graduated with my master's degree, everything was fine and dandy, until Billy's true colors began to show. We would spend so much time together, but when I wanted to get to know the deeper parts of him, he didn't allow it to happen. Those on the outside thought passion and love were there, but in reality, they weren't anymore.

Is marrying him something I regret? Maybe, but I wouldn't be who I am today if I hadn't. I wouldn't have learned so much about my past self and how this experience influenced me if I'd chosen differently.

Over the past five years, our marriage drifted apart. We tried our hardest to fix things between us, but nothing changed. At the beginning of the year, we attempted couples counseling, but even that didn't work.

I always felt like I put more effort into our relationship than he did, and I couldn't figure out why. I have my faults and did some things I shouldn't have during our marriage, but it'd only ever been to try to make me happy when he couldn't. Eventually, Billy decided it was time for us to get a divorce since our relationship had been so strenuous, and I completely agreed with the decision.

The divorce process has been emotionally draining and challenging. When we met with lawyers to determine who would receive what from our marriage, it'd been an easy decision to give him the house because I didn't want much from the marriage. The funds we shared were split down the middle, allowing me to get an apartment for myself.

Every part of the separation sucks, but I know it is worth it in the end because I will get back on my feet, learning to live my life again as a single woman on a single income.

Sitting in my apartment thinking about what the next few weeks will bring, I look at my email hoping for some good news regarding the professor job applications I have put in. I scroll until I come across an email from my alma mater that says, "Congratulations, Mariah White! You have been selected as an Adjunct Professor in the Social Work Department at Redon University."

Shocked, I immediately called my best friend Erin to tell her the good news. The phone rings a few times until she picks up, and before she can speak, I beat her to it.

"Bitch, guess what."

"Let me guess, you have finally gotten over that asshole Billy?" she asks.

Pausing, I think about her question, and while technically, it is true, it isn't why I called. "I received my dream job as a Social Work Professor at Redon University."

Happy screams come from the other end. "Congratulations, hun! I am so happy for you."

We chat for a little while about how I've been doing since the divorce and how I feel about taking on the new role in a couple of months. Part of me is nervous because of my past that I don't want to catch up to me. I know that, if it does, it could not only ruin my career but my life. And while I understand I need to be positive, keep my head up, and not focus on the negative, sometimes those thoughts take over my mind.

As I drift into my fear, Erin pulls me out of it. "So, your dirty thirty is this upcoming weekend. What are the plans? Are we renting a party bus or going to a strip club?"

Consumed by the divorce, thinking about my birthday had become an afterthought. "Maybe we can hit up a few bars and keep it low-key," I say, hoping she'll understand.

As if she's disappointed, a deafening silence lingers from the other end of the phone until she finally replies, "That's fine. I will meet you at your house Saturday night around 6:00 p.m. to get the birthday festivities started."

Knowing her, this means she will arrive a few hours early, expecting me to be ready to go out. But, since I like to take my time getting ready, I plan to do just that. Plus, since it is my day, I shouldn't be rushed to begin with.

With Saturday only a night away, I still can't believe I am about to turn the big three-oh. I didn't picture myself divorced and getting my dream job at this age, but here I am. And since my family always said Billy was too good for me, I isolated myself from them to avoid any more drama or becoming the topic of discussion at every family gathering, which meant they wouldn't attend the celebration.

Their perspective on our relationship was irrelevant to me because they never truly knew what went on between us. Keeping a positive persona got tiring after a while, and I'm to the point where I no longer care what everyone else has to say or think about me. I know my worth and who I am, and if people don't agree with it, then fuck them. They aren't meant to be in my life.

Frustrated, I reach into my nightstand, pulling out my friend to keep me company for the rest of the night. The need of release helps me feel better when I'm in an emotional low, and as I pull my vibrator out of the bag and press it firmly to my clit, I'm reminded that. As it begins to suck the life out of me, I sink further into the feeling, and Boy, do I enjoy it.

With the vibrator pressed to my clit, I insert two fingers inside of me, making the 'come here' motion to stimulate my g-spot. After a few minutes, I feel the pressure build inside of me, causing my legs to shake. Before I know it, my pussy is throbbing as my orgasm rushes through me. I moan in pleasure, wishing it was someone else doing this to me.

Most men I have been with have been just a quick fuck, not caring about getting me off, just as I didn't care about doing the same to them. As long as I felt someone inside of me, it turned me on to a point that I enjoyed more than anything. Maybe it is because of my past trauma or something else entirely, but that was always the route I took to make myself feel again.

A vibrator can only do so much, but somehow, at this moment, it is doing a lot for me. I continue fucking myself with my fingers, using my toy until my body can't take it anymore. And once I reach my peak multiple times, I finally put it back in its bag before drifting into a much-needed slumber.

SCHOOL O
SOCIAL WO

The next morning comes, and it finally settles that it is my big day. I knew I needed to look halfway decent to go out to the bars, and maybe I would find a guy to let loose with.

But I didn't allow myself to get my hopes up.

First, I review my email from yesterday, making note of what is expected of me in the upcoming weeks as an adjunct professor. I begin making my syllabus to send back by the Monday deadline. Creating it comes to me like second nature, and I shoot it off before 3:30 p.m. Closing my computer I sigh, happy that I crossed something off my to-do list that allows me to have plenty of time to prepare for tonight's festivities. I could hear Erin's disap- pointment if she found out that I was working on my birthday, but I had nothing better to do while I waited for her.

Not even five minutes after I set my computer aside, I hear a knock at my door. Before I can even approach it, Erin bursts into the room, heading straight to my bedroom while yelling "Happy Birthday" as I close the door behind her. Her barging in has become a routine I've accepted; she never waits for me to invite her in.

I walk to my bedroom to find her sitting on my bed as she looks at me in confusion. "Why don't you have your outfit out for tonight?" she asks.

"You do realize what time it is, right? We only have two hours before we head out to hit the bars."

Frustrated, she glares at me as she pushes herself up to dart to the closet. Only seconds pass before she pulls out a black strapless dress with silver high heels, demanding that I put them on. I follow her orders, turning to look in the mirror as a dread for what tonight will bring settles in my gut.

"You look beautiful, babe. Hopefully, you can get fucked tonight," she laughs.

Everything that leaves her mouth catches me off guard, and I blush thinking about her even picturing me in bed with a man. I doubt she cares because she is always open about talking about each other's sex lives, even if I hesitate to do so.

Going to the bathroom, I finish my make-up and hair before checking the time to realize it is only 4:00 p.m. I step through the doorway to find Erin right where I left her. "Why are we getting ready so early when we won't be going out for a couple more hours?"

Erin looks at me, grinning slightly. "Actually, we are going out early. I planned out the entire night. Pizza first, bar second, but just know you are in for the night of your life before your real responsibilities get started."

Her words only meant one thing: tonight was going to be wild, but I try to hope for the best of what it brings.

After dinner, we hit up my favorite spot, the Strider Bar, where I know the bartenders and often get drinks for free or a low charge. Happy with Erin's decision, I settle into my excitement to have a great time tonight, not giving a flying fuck about what is going on around me.

You only turn 30 once, so I know I must make the most of it. With no expectations and hoping to have a blast with my girl, my palms meet the front door of Strider's.

Instantly, we spot my favorite bartender making drinks. He nods as we approach, already preparing something special. Sitting on the barstools, he slides my favorite mixed drink over, a Bahama Mama, and asks Erin what she wants. Like the simple woman she is whenever we go out, she opts for a basic beer instead of getting a cocktail.

We chat for a bit, and before I know it, she is dragging me to the dance floor. Unlike most bars around here, this one has more space to get lost in the music, which is why I end up here, to dance and be free.

Like typical friends who go out, we dance together, getting lost in the blaring music. Lost in the beat, I barely feel someone slide behind me, dancing with me to the trending hip-hop song. Paying no mind, I continue moving with the rhythm, looking over to see that Erin has gained a dance partner too. She and I make eye contact, smiling as a cue that we are good with what is going on.

The "Dirty 30" sash hanging around my shoulders has me assuming that's why someone joined me. It was common that, when going out and wearing something that indicated a birthday, people would often celebrate the milestone with the person the day belonged to.

After a bit of dancing, Erin and I head back to the bar to get another round of drinks. Readying to signal for the bartender to get us our usual, I am cut off when the guy behind me offers to pay.

"Happy birthday, beautiful. I am glad I could have a little dance with you tonight." The corner of his mouth lifts with a gentle grin. "I'm Cyrus, by the way."

"I'm Mariah." As any other words aside from my name become impossible, all I can do is smile. Erin nudges me, and I finally spit out, "Thank you for the dance and the drinks as well."

What a lame introduction.

Engaging in conversation- at a bar is not for me, which many find shocking because of my interest in becoming an adjunct professor at a university, a role that requires a lot of talking. On top of that, as a social worker, learning not to be awkward in social settings is essential, but for some reason, I couldn't help myself.

After grabbing my drink, we head back out to the dance floor for a little longer. When I look down at my watch, the hands greet me at the 8:00 p.m. mark, our cue to go to the next spot. Turning to Cyrus and his friend, I tell them we are heading to the Wallen Bar around the corner to have a few more drinks before we head home for the night, extending an invitation for them to join us. Without hesitation, they follow us to the next bar.

Once we are there, different people offer to buy me a few shots and drinks in honor of my displayed celebration. Accepting a few of their offers in between dances, I make sure I don't overdo it because getting home safely and being blackout drunk don't belong in the same sentence. While most people like to celebrate to that extent on milestone birthdays, I am different.

After about two hours at the Wallen Bar, I finally decide to tell Erin I am ready to go home. Glancing between Cyrus and me, she smirks, implying I should take him home with me.

Knowing I only turn 30 once, I throw out the question, "Cyrus, do you want to get out of here with me?"

He smiles widely as if he has been patiently waiting to accept my offer. "Hell yes."

With that, we head back to my apartment to spend the next couple of hours together, and I can only cross my fingers for a nice hookup to end my birthday night.

SCHOOL OF
SOCIAL WO

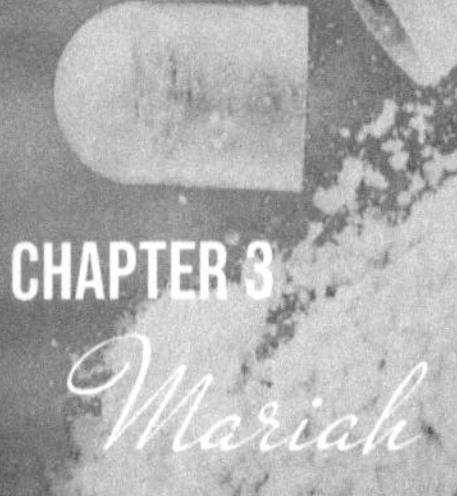

CHAPTER 3

Mariah

arely making it through the front door, our lips meet as our pieces of our clothing begin falling to the floor. Here I was thinking I'd be going home alone tonight to entertain myself with my handy dandy vibrator, but thankfully things are going not according to plan.

Stepping into my room, he instantly kisses down my neck, trailing toward my breasts. In the next second, he unhooks the back of my bra, drawing his tongue across my nipple in one swift motion. Chills slither up my spine as he sucks on it, twirling the other between his fingertips.

Damn. I love how this feels and how much time he is spending on pleasing me. And as he continues moving down my body and pulls off my thong in one swift motion, I'm reminded that it's been a while since I've experienced something like this.

With one flick, he licks across my clit and center, his eyes lifting to meet mine. "Damn, you taste so sweet, and I love your clit piercing."

As he gets lost in pleasing me, my body starts shaking with an intensity I'd never experienced before, not even with my ex-husband. Driven by my pleasure, he inserts two fingers into my pussy and fucks me as fast and deep as he can with them.

Sheesh.

"I am so close," I whimper, prompting him to keep going until my orgasm breaks.

I begin to kiss him again and know that I want to see what I am working with under his clothes. I pull Cyrus's pants and underwear down, needing to please him how he just pleased me. As his length springs free, I realize how thick he is, a little worried that he might not fit when he fucks me. My eyes explore him further, catching sight of his Prince Albert piercing. Never having slept with a pierced man before, I knew this would be a new experience.

Without hesitation, I lick up and down his shaft before I take his head into my mouth. Bobbing with a slow pace, I stroke him with my hand. Once I find my rhythm, I pick up my pace, and before I know it, he takes control.

He grips my hair tightly, fucking my throat. Matching his intensity, I squeeze his balls, feeling him tense up as he nears the edge of his orgasm. Before I know it, his cum drains into my mouth, and I savor every drop of it. He instantly pulls me up and kisses me passionately, causing him to get hard again. I have no idea how he is ready again.

Reaching for his pants pocket, he pulls out a condom. With a familiar, quick motion, he rips the wrapper open. With one hand, he slides the condom down his length, the other circling the bud of my clit. He toys with me briefly until he is satisfied, and then, without warning, he pushes the head of his dick into my entrance.

"You're so big," I gasp, overwhelmed by his length.

He ignores my comment, thrusting deeper into me until he finds his pace.

"Your pussy is so tight. I love how it grips me," he moans, the admiration in his words blooming the heat in my stomach.

Picking up his pace, Cyrus begins to fuck me faster and harder. As I get lost in his thrusts, his fingers wrap around my neck. Slowly and carefully, he finds his grip, squeezing just enough to bring me over the edge with pleasure. My pussy pulsates around his dick as he continues his rhythm, clinging to my throat with every intention of making me cum.

With stars lining my vision, my sudden ability to breathe freely catches me off guard, but not as much as him flipping me over. On my knees with my ass in the air, he pushes into my pussy from behind, thrusting into me as if it were a punishment. Rolling his hips forward a few more times, he cums for a second time, and I join him.

When he pulls out, he goes to the bathroom, grabbing a washcloth to clean me up. With a gentleness I've never experienced, he wipes it across my skin, admiring me with every touch.

Such a gentleman.

Once he is done, he pulls me into a hug, and I sink into him with a sigh, "That was definitely the highlight of my night."

He kisses my forehead, chuckling in a way that has my heart heating. "I'm glad I was able to give you such a memorable gift for your birthday."

We lay there in silence, basking in one another's presence. What feels like only five minutes goes by before I notice how late it is. Running my fingers across his chest, I push myself up to look at him. "I would love for you to be here longer, but it is about time for me to get ready for bed."

Even as he realizes I am kicking him out, he

places a gentle kiss to my forehead. "Thank you for being the highlight of my night, hopefully I will see you around again at some point."

Putting his clothes on, I watch him, mapping out his body before I push myself up from the bed. I walk him to the front door, locking it behind him when he steps outside.

The following day, the only thing I can think about is Cyrus. I can't believe how much fun I had with him and how many orgasms he gave me without me having to ask. It was a hookup that we kept moving, not asking one another too many questions or exchanging phone numbers.

But part of me hopes I see him around because it was a good fuck, a night I wouldn't be mad about experiencing again.

for wha
to be be
point o
Blackn
obtain
by th
expos

CHAPTER 4

Cyrus

I've always kept to myself, and since I don't go out often, most people describe me as a home-body. I prefer to chill with my friends and play video games, but sometimes, you can find me reading a thriller novel, depending on what mood I am in.

My decision to go out to the bar for once isn't something I regret. I enjoyed my time with Sean and meeting the new girl Mariah, and while getting laid wasn't necessarily at the forefront of my mind last night, I'm glad it happened. It was nice to get my dick sucked, but that hadn't been my priority. I loved pleasing a woman, and being able to spend time on her body would have been enough to satisfy me.

Even after finding out that I was younger than

her, she still enjoyed everything I could offer. Every sound she made stayed in my mind, and I couldn't help but consider what I would have done with her if we had gone another round. I'd be lying if I said I wasn't a little bummed when she kicked me out, but I also respect the fact that not everybody wants a guy who they just met spending the night.

Serving today at the local seafood restaurant, I suppose her decision to send me on my way had been for the better. If I had stayed any longer, I definitely would have called out, which would have backfired because I need the money.

As I get ready to head to the restaurant for my shift, I replay what Mariah and I did last night. I need to see her again, and fear that if I don't, these thoughts will consume me. The limited information I have about her makes finding her on social media to befriend her difficult, and ultimately, I don't really know what to do to find her.

I get to my car, pull up Instagram, and look up the name Mariah. Thousands of people come up, but she isn't one of them, meaning she either doesn't have social media or her profile is private. The idea of returning to Strider Bar after my shift tonight sounds appealing, especially if it gives me the chance to see if she's a regular. I just need to make it through my shift before I figure out what to do next, which became impossible because of how slow it was.

Guess people don't always want seafood for lunch on a Sunday. I picked up this extra shift, because I could use a little extra money, but this time on a Sunday doesn't work well. I make a mental note of this for the next time someone asks me if I want their lunch shift because it needs to be worth it in order for me to take it.

After my shift, I stop by my house for a quick shower. The last thing I want is to smell like seafood at a bar, and I ensure that doesn't happen by freshening up further with some nice and woodsy cologne.

The street to Strider Bar is practically empty, which I suppose makes sense because most people in town don't go to the bar on Sunday. Pushing the door open, I make my way inside, greeted by the smell of ale with a little cigarette smoke. As soon as I get to the bar, I request a beer, making small talk with the bartender for a little.

After an hour goes by, I realize she isn't coming, and decide to head home. Part of me considers stopping by her apartment on the way, but the other sways me not to because of how creepy it would come across.

Sean is sitting on the couch when I return to the apartment, and the only thing that's bad about having him as a roommate is how nosy he can be. When I returned from Mariah's, I hadn't seen him, and somehow avoided him before work, so I know he will have something to say.

He looks at me, the question I'd expected coming from him. "So, how did the rest of the night go with the girl from the bar? I didn't even hear you get home."

Going to the kitchen, I pour myself a neat bourbon before planting myself on the couch beside him. "It was really good but I didn't get any of her information, so I'm unsure if I will see her again."

Disappointment floods his face, clearly expecting more details, and I continue, "I mean, I'm a big enough fool that I went back there after work to see if she'd be there."

"Damn, Cy, it was one night, and you are already on the hunt for her?" he laughs.

I roll my eyes, changing the subject because I can't do this with him right now. We talk a little about if there are any upcoming plans for the weekend and if we want to have a party or something at the apartment.

Knowing I have a lot of shifts coming up to make as much money as possible, I spend the rest of the day relaxing. With work slowing down and my focus shifting elsewhere, it's a temporary sacrifice I know I need to make, just as I know I need to make the most out of the brief downtime as I have.

SCHOOL O
SOCIAL WO

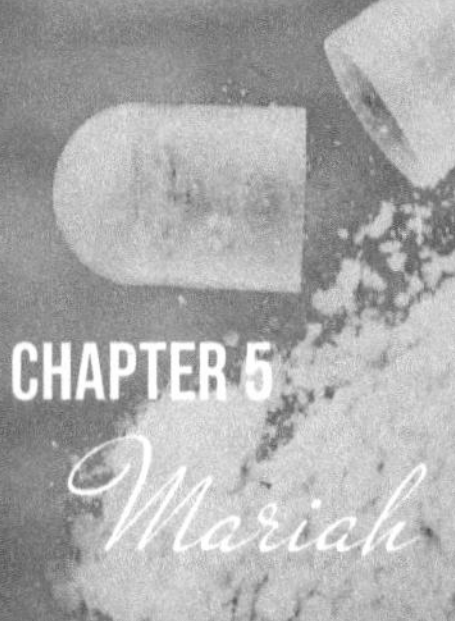

CHAPTER 5

Mariah

With a week left until I start teaching classes at the university, I need to crack down and focus on getting everything in place before reality sets in. Being entrusted to help students learn the necessary skills and social work competencies to begin their career in the field, I know I can't screw this up. There is nothing I can let get in the way of the start of the job I have always wanted.

A family friend told me that starting in a different area of the college could help pave the way to becoming a professor, and that is precisely what happened to me. I am grateful that I listened to her because I wouldn't be where I am today if I hadn't.

I would be lying if I said I wasn't a little nervous about whether the students will gravitate toward my learning style considering I am new to the professor world and younger than most of the professors I had when I was still in school.

Where older professors possess a wealth of knowledge and experience within the field, a fresh face like me relies on what I learned through my internships and research. And while I do believe I will be a good asset to Redon University, I need to build my confidence to ensure that I am not setting myself or others up for failure.

This semester, I am assigned to teach a community relations course, which is right up my alley. When I worked in student support, I volunteered in social work roles within similar settings, which helped me gain more knowledge of the field and some of the members' needs. With this under my belt, and all I have learned through the interactions I experienced, I feel I will succeed in teaching the subject. Not only that, but the coursework throughout undergraduate and graduate school will be an added bonus to connect students' learning to the core social work competencies.

Taking a short break from focusing on lesson planning, I order my go-to meal from my favorite Chinese spot: beef and broccoli with a bit of spicy peppers added to it.

While waiting for it to be delivered, I head to the kitchen, pulling out a bottle of dry red wine. Out of nowhere, my thoughts return to last night, and I can't help but picture Cyrus back in my apartment and the earth-shattering orgasms he gave me.

I don't know why I keep thinking about it because the men I hook up with are never memorable. I often move on, never revisiting what they did to me or how they made me feel. But, for some reason, I can't get this man out of my head, and I know I need to because of the distraction he will cause in the future.

Interrupting my train of thought, my doorbell rings. I pull myself together, inhaling deeply before I head to the door, contemplating how quick their delivery time felt today when it usually takes forever.

I sit and eat at the dinner table, sipping on my glass of wine while I scroll on Instagram. Landing on a photo of one of my high school friends, a broad smile covers her face, each photo showing her reaction to an unexpected proposal. I can't help but stumble back to my engagement on the cruise ship and think about how I should have waited a little longer to commit myself to someone like that. If I had, then maybe a divorce wouldn't have happened, even though I am more to blame for our separation than Billy.

"Hopefully it works out for them," I mutter to myself, gulping down the rest of my wine because of how messy things became between me and Billy. I have changed my ways since, and the last thing I want is for those thoughts or actions to resurface.

Luckily, my phone rings, and I look down to see Erin's name on the screen. It has become routine for us to have our nightly calls to decompress from the day and check in with one another.

We met at Redon University, where she works in the admissions department. Becoming close friends in such a short period made me think it was fate that we met because of how instantly we clicked. Between being big book lovers and red wine drinkers, I am grateful to be able to call her my best friend.

I pick up the phone, Erin's sweet voice flooding my ear. "How has the lesson planning been going today? I know you wanted to get as much of it done as possible so you can have a bit of a break before classes start."

Feeling like an overachiever because of the amount of work I did today, I reply, "I got everything in place for the first two weeks of classes, and I'm honestly shocked. I guess it's true when they say that sitting down and focusing on something you enjoy motivates you to knock out as much work as possible."

"Damn girl! I would be lying if I said I wasn't surprised, but I am proud of how much you were able to get done. I know once you set your mind to completing a task, you will do whatever it takes to complete it," she says, her words meaning more to me than I could ever explain.

We continue to chat for a bit about school and random things until it is time to head to bed. We say our goodnights, and I do my nightly routine before falling into a steady and peaceful sleep.

SCHOOL O
SOCIAL WO

Mariah

Today is the first day of classes. I wake up early to get dressed and make myself look presentable for the day. After curling my hair, I put on slacks with a floral blouse. I have never been one for heels unless forced by Erin, so I opt out of wearing them and put on some flats instead. I continue with my morning routine by making my favorite coffee with French vanilla creamer in it, grabbing a chocolate protein shake for the road.

When I get to Redon University, I park in the same lot I used when I was in student support. One of the perks of being an adjunct professor is that I teach one class in the same classroom daily, so there isn't a risk of me having to navigate other buildings. Having been a student here myself, I already know the campus well.

I head to my office, located in the same building as my classroom, to enjoy my breakfast and ensure I have enough syllabi printed out for the day. With this class having fifteen students, I am grateful because I couldn't imagine starting my teaching career with thirty or more students. Smaller classes help professors build connections with students, making it easier to remember them by name.

At my desk, I look through the list of students, and a familiar name appears: *Cyrus*. This can't be the same Cyrus I met the other night, the one who did unimaginable things to me. If it is, it would be the biggest conflict of interest in my career.

We never talked about work, and I hadn't asked his age. All I knew was that he had to be over twenty-one because he could drink at both bars. This town is strict about not serving anyone under-age, and always seems to catch when someone is using a fake ID.

My head starts to spin as memories of that night pop up again. This can't be happening. I hope and pray this is not the same Cyrus from the other night, and that it is just a coincidence that someone shares the same name as him.

for wha
to be be
point o
Blackn
obtain
by thr
expos

CHAPTER 7

Cyrus

After taking some time off from school, I'm finally back. It's the first day of classes, and I am one step closer to receiving my bachelor's degree in social work. I chose this field because there aren't many men who are social workers, and so many men are struggling with social issues and mental health concerns. My hope is to make a difference, helping those who are homeless. It's something I know I can connect with them on a different level than most social workers.

When I was fifteen, my family struggled financially. We couldn't keep up with the bills, and eventually, we were evicted. While my parents worked to save enough for us to get back on our feet, we spent time in a homeless shelter, and I met a social worker who changed my life. From then on, I knew this was the path I wanted to follow.

After my senior year of high school, I took a gap year to work and save money before looking into colleges. I applied for local schools and got accepted into a Bachelor of Social Work program at Redon University. The moment I saw the acceptance letter, I knew I wanted to follow through.

Fast forward to now—I'm in my senior year, just a step away from graduating. This semester, I only have three courses: Abnormal Psychology, Community Relations, and a practicum. Of the three, Community Relations excites me the most, since it ties into the work I want to pursue.

But since I picked up as many shifts as I could before classes started, I'm exhausted. Unsure how awake I'll be, I grab an energy drink and head to my car to start my journey to school.

Since it is my last year, I opted to live off-campus in an apartment ten minutes away. Turning on the radio to the country station, I let the music carry me through my short commute.

I arrive about thirty minutes early and check my schedule to see I have Community Relations first with Professor White. I have always been the type of person who shows up early, even when I don't need to. On the first day, it feels especially important and gives me time to find the classroom, settle in, and select the perfect seat.

Before class starts, I head to the cafeteria for a quick breakfast, and then make my way to the lecture hall.

SCHOOL OF
SOCIAL WO

Five minutes before class, students begin trickling in. My nerves spike as I notice not all fifteen have arrived. Sitting behind my desk, I focus on steadying my breath, reminding myself that I am excited. This class has the potential to be a lot of fun, but the one name on my roster—Cyrus—makes me very nervous.

I keep my eyes on my laptop, scrolling through emails to make sure I am not missing any essential upcoming meetings or important messages. Nothing. A glance at the clock tells me it's 10:00 a.m., which means it's time to begin.

Pushing back from the desk, I rise and scan the room. Then my gaze locks with someone it never should have. *Cyrus.* The name on my roster is the same as the man I hooked up with a week ago on my birthday. My stomach drops. This could jeopardize everything. For a split second, I cling to the hope that maybe he won't remember me. But who am I kidding? I remember him too well.

I clear my throat and greet the class. "Good morning. My name is Professor White, and I'll be teaching Community Relations this semester. I am glad you all registered for this course, and I'm excited to get to know you while we explore the community and our role as social workers in the field."

Some students seem more eager to be here, while others already seem checked out. I suppose some registered for the class simply to fulfill a requirement for graduation.

I start by taking roll, and one by one, students respond until I reach the very last name on the list— of course it would be at the end of the alphabet. "Cyrus Valentine."

He raises his hand. "That's me."

My heart slams against my ribs.

I can't believe this is happening. He's actually in my class. Forcing the thoughts aside, I move through the rows, handing a syllabus to each student. We take time reviewing expectations for the semester, and I answer a few questions, which only takes up thirty minutes of class.

Since today is syllabus day, I let the class out early, and of course, Cyrus stays back. My stomach knots because I don't want to have this conversation. I'd rather pretend the other night never happened, but I know I need to address it. It was a one-time thing that cannot happen again.

He approaches my desk, standing too close, forcing me to take a step back.

"Hey, beautiful, I have been thinking about you since the night we met," he says.

This cannot be how this starts. He can't miss me, and he can't continue to think about me. If he does, everything only gets messier. This is my first year as a professor, and if something happens again, my career could be over before it begins.

"Please address me as Professor White," I say firmly. "I know we had a good time the other night, but it cannot happen again. That was a one-time mistake. If I had known you were my student, it never would have happened in the first place. From now on, our relationship must stay professional, nothing more."

Disappointment flashes across his face, but it needed to be said. "What people don't know won't hurt them," he counters. "We can keep it our little secret."

I take another step back, my voice sharper. "Cyrus, I'm serious. Drop it. I am your professor, and will not engage in any kind of relationship with a student of mine."

I don't know how much clearer I can be with him; it's like nothing I say is clicking.

"You're going to regret telling me no," he mutters, storming to the door and slamming it shut behind him.

I sit frozen for a moment, stunned. Why is he so angry? It was just a one-night stand, and there was nothing more to it.

Dropping back into my chair, I force myself through deep breathing exercises, trying to ground my anxiety. His behavior feels unhinged, and the thought of seeing him makes my skin crawl. Part of me wonders if I can have him moved to another class, but since I'm the only one teaching this course, pulling him out would feel unfair.

No matter what, I'll have to grit my teeth, keep the boundary firm, and do my best to maintain a professional relationship with him.

What I don't like is the way he threatened me. Part of me knows I should report it to the school leadership, but fear holds me back. What if they fire me before I even get a chance to prove myself? I hadn't known he was a student at the time, but still, the whole situation feels like a trap. After I think about it a little longer, I decide to hold off. If it escalates further, then I will act.

Needing to talk about it, I head to the admissions office to see if Erin is in. Luckily, she is. I knock on her door, and she greets me with a smile. Stepping inside her office, I close the door behind me, and sink into the chair across from her.

"Erin, the craziest thing happened in my class today, and I don't know what to do," I say.

She studies me closely, waiting, giving me space to continue.

"Well," I exhale, "the guy I met at the Strider Bar... turns out he's one of my students."

Erin's eyes widen, and she slaps her hand over her mouth. "What are you going to do? I know you enjoyed what happened between the two of you, but he is your student—you can't do anything further with him."

"I know," I admit, my voice low. "I told him it was a one-time thing, and he seemed frustrated. He told me I'd regret telling him that, and now I don't know what to think."

We continued to talk about it for a little while, her concern steady as I try to make sense of the situation. Eventually, I head home, desperate to clear my mind. I draw a bath and sink into the water, letting the steam soften the tension from the day. At least I don't have office hours tomorrow; one small relief. It means I can avoid the Cyrus mess until class resumes on Wednesday.

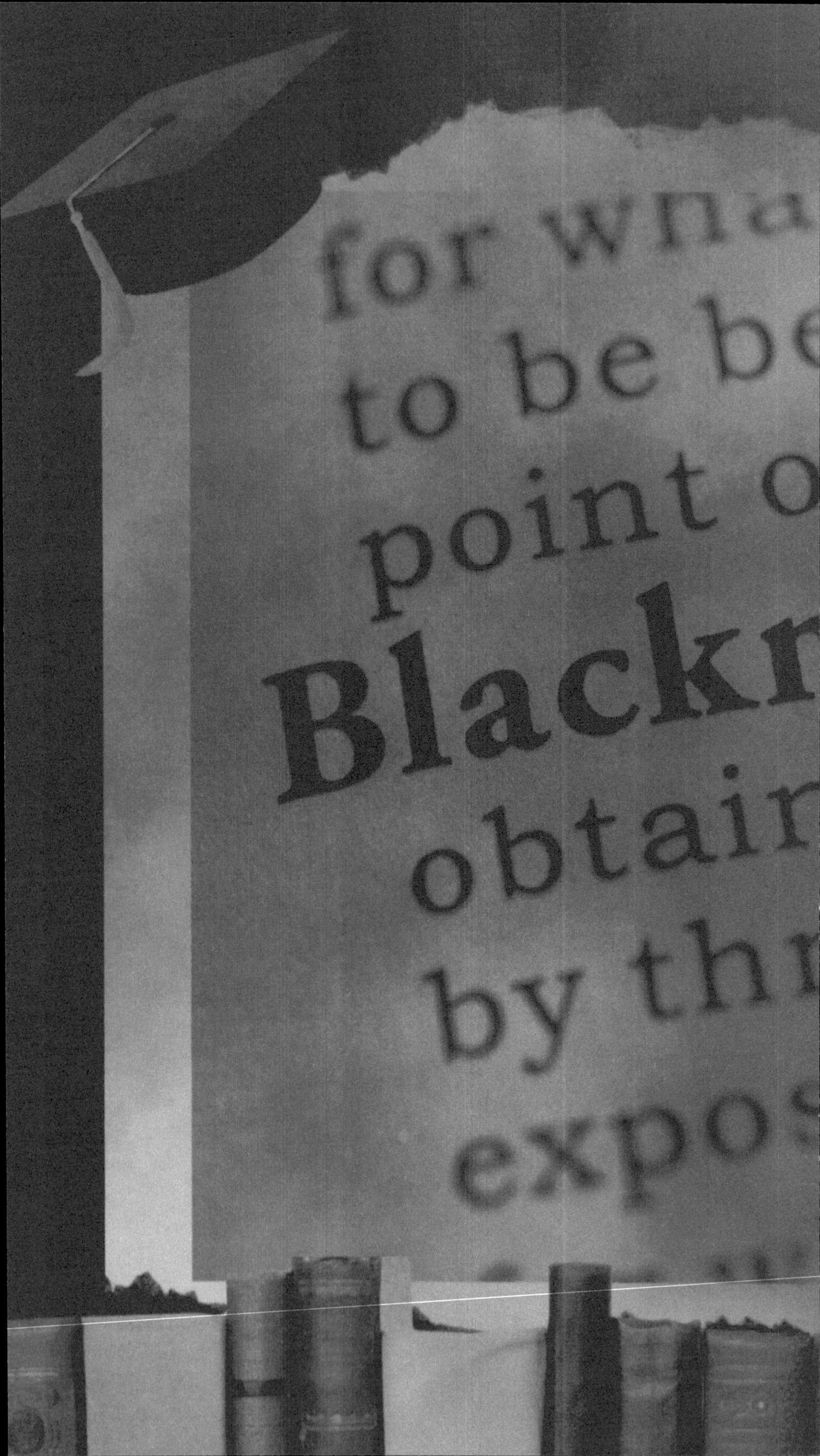

for wha
to be be
point o
Black
obtain
by th
expos

CHAPTER 9

Cyrus

When I get home, I'm still reeling. The Mariah I met during summer break is my professor. I've never seen her around campus before but then again, I usually keep to myself—straight to class, straight home. Her name has never been on the roster of social work professors before, which means she must be new. If she's going to be in my life, I need to do some digging on her to figure out more of her background and what she is all about.

I call my older brother, Joe. He owes me a favor after I helped him out a few years ago, and he's the kind of guy who can get information others can't. He's a lawyer, and pretty damn good at his job.

After a few rings, he finally answers, his voice filled with frustration. "Cyrus, what do you want?

You disappear for a year and then call me out of the blue. Let me guess; you need something."

So that's how he wants to start this conversation. I could put him on blast and air out his dirty laundry, but I swallow the urge and keep my tone even. "Hey, Joe. I was calling to cash in my favor. I need you to look into someone for me."

He sighs loudly through the receiver, so I continue, "I have a professor named Mariah White. I need you to dig up any information you can on her and send it to me."

I sense doubt coming from him, but he eventually replies, "Give me a couple of days. I'll see what I can find. I need to check for any aliases too. Can you at least give me a description in case photos pop up under her name?"

"All I know is she has brunette hair, brown eyes, average build. I believe this is her first year teaching at Redon University. She just turned thirty before the school year started, and…" I pause, then add, "I've been to her apartment. I'll send you the address."

With that, he hangs up, alredy shifting into work mode.

Maybe I am crazy for going this far, but I can't help myself—I need to know more about her. She is so mysterious, and I hate the way she brushed me off like she didn't want anything to do with me. She wants to pretend what happened between us meant nothing, but I don't buy that. I feel connected to her, stronger than anything I've felt before, and I'll make sure I get more.

Whether she wants it or not.

I know it will take Joe a few days to dig up information on Mariah, but the wait makes me restless. I can't just sit around, so I lace up my shoes and head toward her apartment.

As I arrive, I spot her pulling into the lot in her blue car, parking directly in front of her building. I watch as she walks toward her unit, unlocks the door, and disappears inside. Once I'm sure she's gone, I sneak over to her car, snap a photograph of her license plate, and send it to Joe in hopes it speeds up the process.

Some people would call me crazy. Some might even say I'm a stalker. But that's not how I see it. I'm just curious. Drawn in. When I first laid my eyes on her, it felt like love at first sight, and that isn't something I can just put behind me.

There's something about her that sends blood rushing to my dick, growing with the need to devour her. Hurrying back to my apartment, I head straight to the shower, stroking myself at the thought of her. I can't help but moan her name as I pick up the pace, not stopping until my cum shoots down the drain.

I get out of the shower, dry off, and collapse into bed, my mind drumming with anticipation. Sleep comes slowly, pulling me under with the restless question of what Joe will uncover about Mariah.

JOE

I knew the day would come when my brother called in the favor I owed him. I thought it would be a brutal request, but it turns out he only wants me to dig into one of his professors. Easy enough. He's even made it easier by handing over details that would be hard to track down otherwise. With that information, I start with a basic database search. Almost immediately, I get a couple hits; one under Mariah White, another under Mariah Harrington.

It doesn't take long to piece it together. Mariah Harrington was her married name, before a recent divorce finalized this year. The records are sealed, which means only Mariah, her ex-husband Billy, and the layers involved know the full story.

Still, what I can access paints a messy picture. The filings suggest Billy filed on grounds of infidelity and drug use. The paperwork claims Mariah had been abusing narcotics, though the extent wasn't spelled out. Apparently, Billy agreed not to involve law enforcement as long as she cooperated and kept the divorce amicable.

By the looks of it, the drugs weren't legal, which raises a red flag. A part of me hesitates; if I hand this over to Cyrus, he could use it in the wrong way. But a favor is a favor, and if he suspects I'm holding back, he'll find out regardless.

I keep combing through the records, and everything appears to be in order. Mariah holds a master's degree in social work and has been working at Redon University for a while now, though this is her first year as a professor. Her vehicle and apartment are listed in her name, and there's no record of any legal trouble. Maybe that clean slate is what allowed her to step into her position. If the truth of the divorce surfaced, I doubt she'd be where she is today.

A few days later, I reach out to Cyrus, asking him to meet me at a local diner. I slide into the booth with a manila folder in hand and say, "Thank you for making my job easier by sending me all the information I needed to track her down. I have compiled everything I could find. Just don't do anything reckless with it."

He smirks, and that expression tells me more than his words ever could. "Thank you for putting this together for me. Don't worry about what I will do with it."

As soon as I pass the manila folder to him, I get up and prepare to leave the diner. Just as I turn, he says, "I will reach out to you more often. I miss talking to you and having that brotherly bond."

I shake my head, unconvinced. I'll believe it when I see it.

for wha
to be be
point o
Black
obtain
by thr
expos

CHAPTER 10

Cyrus

When I get home, I head straight to my bedroom and close the door so Sean can't bother me. I go through the manila folder of information Joe gathered on Mariah. To my surprise, there aren't many pages inside, which means he didn't find a lot on her. Maybe that's a good thing.

As I flip through, a sticky note catches my eye: *Classified information, please do not share.* Strange. If Joe included it here, shouldn't it all be usable?

The flagged documents turn out to be about Mariah's divorce. I never realized she had been married. Reading closer, I notice the split was due to infidelity and drug use. Her ex-husband had promised not to tell anyone about it to keep her out of trouble, but it makes me wonder how serious it was.

I keep this information tucked in the back of my mind, as it may come in handy later. Nothing else in the paperwork stands out, so I slide it back in the manila folder and place it in a drawer for safekeeping. With that, I decide to call it a night, eager to see her in class tomorrow.

The following day comes, and I follow my usual routine, getting ready to head to campus. I've always liked how my schedule stacks everything on Mondays, Wednesdays, and Fridays. It gives me days off in between, and more chances to see Mariah.

Before leaving, I slip the manila folder into my backpack, and head to my car. When I told Mariah she was going to regret turning me down, I meant it. With this kind of information, she won't be able to avoid me. I won't address it at school today. But after? She won't have a choice.

Running late, I pull up at the school and head straight to the classroom. I decide to play it cool while in class, but planned to stay behind again to have another little conversation with Mariah. She acts so innocent in front of everyone, but I know she has a dark side.

I'd hate to expose what I know, but if she won't cooperate, I will make her life a living hell. Wouldn't it suck if her dreams of being a professor were ruined by damning information presented to the school administrators? It doesn't bother me—I'll do whatever it takes.

She's going to be mine, one way or another.

SCHOOL O
SOCIAL WO

CHAPTER 11

Mariah

I t's Wednesday, which means I'm stuck seeing Cyrus again. I should have made better choices the night of my birthday, but I just wanted to have fun. I never thought it would land me in this situation.

I paste a smile on my face, focusing on getting through class.. Today is our get-to-know-one-another session, where students share their experiences with community work. It's one of my favorite days of the semester because connection matters in this field, and hearing their goals helps me create lessons that will aid their success in the future.

All fifteen students showed up, and the conversations between them were much more lively. Everyone seemed so open to sharing more about themselves. It gave me a clear picture of what drives them and how I can guide their learning.

The fifty-minute class flew by today, but I noticed one student in particular staying back after class again. *Cyrus.* I don't understand what he wants; it's only the second day, and we haven't even dug into any real coursework.

"Hey, Professor White," he says casually, like we're old friends. "Meet me at the Strider Bar at five tonight. We need to talk."

He is more direct today, and I hesitate, realizing he doesn't comprehend what a 'one-time thing' meant.

"Cyrus, I told you we cannot meet outside of class. I am your professor, and meeting at a bar is not professional."

His brain just isn't clicking anymore, and it is really pissing me off. Anger etches across his face, like he's offended I'd even try to tell him we cannot meet.

"You don't really have a choice," he says flatly. "I have something that you need to see, and I can't bring it up here at the university. It needs to be somewhere else."

I don't know what he's holding over me, or why it can't be said here. Against my better judgement, I give in, hoping it will end this charade.

"Fine. I'll be there. But this is the only time, Cyrus. The *only* time. So whatever it is, it better be worth it."

He smirks. "We'll see about that."

Then he walks out, my pulse pounding a mile a minute, dread twisting through me as I think about how this meeting will go.

SCHOOL O
SOCIAL WO

CHAPTER 12

Mariah

After class, I head to my office, replaying the interaction with Cyrus. Whatever he wants to say, he's convinced it can't be done here. I should have stood my ground, insisted the conversation needed to stay within school walls. But the look in his eyes made it clear there was no room for debate.

I sit down at my desk, answering emails and checking to make sure I haven't missed any important announcements. I stay, going through the motions of office hours until 1:00 p.m. The time drags, maybe because of the anticipation of what's to come.

When my office hours finally end, I head home to eat a late lunch, shower, and read a little before going to the Strider Bar. Dark romance has always been my escape; I can tear through ten books a month when I'm not buried in work, but even now my escape feels minor. I get lost in my book, and before I realize it, my 4:30 alarm goes off, reminding me I need to get myself together to meet with him.

I get to the Strider Bar, spotting Cyrus already tucked into a booth in the corner. A beer sits in front of him, and across from it is my classic Bahama Mama that I got the day I met him. It's sweet he remembers my order, but having a drink with a student is wildly inappropriate.

I slide into the booth, and he pushes the glass toward me.

"The drink is safe. I didn't do anything to it, if that is what you are worried about," he says smugly.

The thought hadn't even crossed my mind. Until now.

"It's not that," I state, shoving the glass back at him. "It's the fact that it isn't appropriate to drink with you. Especially in person. Why am I even here?"

His expression darkens so abruptly it makes me nervous. For a moment, all I think about is if I did something wrong to frustrate him, or if this is just who he is. He stares at me, chugging his beer, and the silence stretches long enough to make me feel like this is a waste of my time.

Finally, he leans forward. "I had some digging done on you, and I found some damning information. Things I doubt you'd want released to the public."

I'm confused. There shouldn't be any information that someone should be able to gather, unless they are a part of the legal system. My past was buried, and the only people who should know the truth are Billy, our lawyers, and me.

He has to be lying to get a reaction out of me, so I play it off like I don't know what he's talking about. "There's nothing you could have found that would be incriminating. I've had a good life, no run-ins with the law, so I don't really know what you are trying to hold over me."

He shakes his head, making me feel like he truly knows about my past. His finger taps against his chin as if he's deciding where to begin.

Finally, the silence breaks. "I know about your divorce with Billy Harrington. Don't try denying it. I won't release it if you agree to go on dates with me. We can meet here, the town over, or even at one of our apartments. This isn't negotiable. If you don't comply, I'll make sure this information ruins your career before it even starts."

My jaw drops. Blackmail. He's actually black-mailing *me*.. If word about my drug use gets out,

Redon University would cut ties with me in a heartbeat.

"How am I supposed to believe what you are saying?" I manage to ask.

Instantly, he pulls out a manila folder and slides it towards me. I open it and take out the contents, and of course, the first thing I see is my divorce records. I have no clue how he found this.

"Fine," I snap, closing the folder. "But these dates will not happen in public. No one can see me with you because that will tarnish my career."

I can't believe I agreed to this, but I finally have the career I want, and I cannot let him destroy it. He asks for my phone, and reluctantly hand it over, watching as he inputs his phone number before asking for mine in return.

"We will be in touch," he says, sliding out of the booth and walking away.

I make my way to the bar counter and ask for a shot of vodka. Throwing it back with one gulp, I leave a twenty behind and head for my apartment.

My mind is reeling. He uncovered secrets I thought were buried for good, and I need to figure out how.

LOUNGE

for wha

to be be
point o

Blackn

obtain

by thr

expos

CHAPTER 13

Cyrus

That was easier than I expected. The confusion on her face said it all; she couldn't wrap her mind around how I'd gotten my hands on that information. Little does she know I have connections in places where obtaining access to records that others cannot easily find is easy.

I am thankful to have the hookup. Without it, I wouldn't have the leverage to make her agree. Blackmail was never the goal, because I don't want to ruin her life. I just want her to care for me the way that I care for her.

She probably thinks I'm a creep, but it's just because I have had strong feelings for her since we met. Call me crazy, but it is normal for instant love to happen. Maybe I am a little obsessed, too, but she doesn't need to know that.

I want what is mine, which is her, even if she doesn't realize it yet. We will see how long it takes before she does.

I pull out my phone, hunting for her contact card. My fingers move quickly.

Hey, beautiful. Let's meet up tomorrow at noon at Roger's Diner in town. I know you said you don't want to meet in public places, but I don't care. I don't have classes, and it is your day off from school, so it would be perfect.

I ache with anticipation about what she is going to say. Three dots appear, then vanish. Why is she playing me? Doesn't she know I need the confirmation and reassurance she'll be there?

See you then.

Short. Too short. I want to send her another message because I want more, but I don't want to seem too obsessed. At least not yet. I'll let it build.

SCHOOL O
SOCIAL WO

CHAPTER 14

Mariah

The man has seriously lost his mind. If he doesn't get his way, he'll blackmail me, which would destroy me. My only real choice is to comply. Maybe it won't be too bad, as long as no one else finds out about us meeting up.

I was shocked he didn't get mad when I replied with such a short message after he asked me to meet up tomorrow. It is what it is. I need to play his game until I can either shut him down or find something incriminating to use against him. I have some power over whether he passes or fails the Community Relations class, but I don't want to stoop to his level. Maybe this arrangement won't last too long, and he'll forget about it sooner rather than later.

When I get home, I call Erin and ask her to come over so we can talk and drink a bottle of wine. She happily agrees, even though we have work tomorrow.

When she gets to my apartment, I've already set two glasses of wine on the kitchen table, ready for us to sit down and get straight to business.

"So, I met with Cyrus today..." I start, but Erin cuts me off instantly, yelling, "WHAT?"

I probably should have eased her into the conversation, but I just needed to rip the Band-Aid off. Even if it sounded bad, I needed to get it out.

I take a deep breath before continuing. "It isn't what you think. He wouldn't leave me alone and forced me to meet with him. It was that or he was going to use my past to blackmail me. I wish I could tell you more about everything, but I just can't right now. All I can say is that he wants me to do exactly what he says, or he will expose what happened and the information regarding my divorce. I can't let that happen."

Tears sting my eyes, and Erin pulls me in for a hug. "Breathe in and breathe out, hun. It will be okay, and I will be here to support you through whatever you need."

I wish her words would calm me, but I feel so overwhelmed with the unknown of what could happen with Cyrus. I want to comply with him to protect everything I've built, but I could still ruin it all if it gets out that I am seeing him. Nobody will understand why I am following his orders—no one except Erin.

I have to find a way to stay positive and hopeful, even if it's just for myself.

After talking with Erin for a while, we put on a movie, and at some point I dozed off. All of the crying must have worn me out.

When I wake, the clock reads 2:00 a.m., and Erin is gone. I get up and walk to the kitchen to get a glass of water, noticing a note from her on the table.

I really appreciate her and her support. Now I just need to find the courage to tell her what is happening. I'm scared she'll judge me, but part of me believes I can trust her and open up without it turning into something negative. Maybe I just need to sleep on it and see if it is the right thing to do.

After I chug down my glass of water, I head to the bedroom. Within seconds of lying down, I drift back off to sleep.

SCHOOL O
SOCIAL WO

CHAPTER 15

Mariah

Being married to my college sweetheart was always a dream. Billy treats me well, cooks for me, and takes me shopping whenever I want. On the surface, he's perfect. But behind closed doors, I have concerns.

Sex seems to be the last thing on his mind when it comes to me. Whenever I try to initiate, he always complains about being tired or not being in the mood. It's a huge red flag. In the beginning, we would fuck like jackrabbits and had a wonderful sex life, but over the past year, it's like the interest has disappeared.

My vibrator has basically become my best friend. When he stays up all night gaming, I pull it out and give myself the release he won't.

Tonight, he's lying next to me in bed. I kiss him,

hoping maybe this time will be different— two months without sex is killing me. But as usual, he doesn't give in. So I reach into my nightstand drawer, grab my toy, and slide my panties down, tossing them to the side. The buzz against my clit fills the silence, and I let myself unravel.

Part of me hopes he'll join in, but instead, this asshole gets up and walks out to the living room. This infuriates me. He's my husband; shouldn't he want to touch me, help me, *something?* But I thought wrong. Ten minutes and several orgasms later, he still hasn't come back to bed, so I turn the toy off and doze off in a slumber.

By mid-morning the next day, I walk out into the living room and find Billy curled up in a blanket, still asleep. I am so pissed off that I want to scream at him, but I know that won't make anything better, so I end up going back into the bedroom to get ready for the day.

Once I'm dressed, I realize I don't want to be in this house with someone who doesn't want me. Instead, I want to go out and have a little fun to take my mind off the rejection I constantly receive from him. I go to the coffee shop to get my morning coffee and a bagel because I have about an hour before I can get something stronger at any of the local bars.

While I am sitting and drinking my Caramel

Macchiato, a reckless thought comes to my mind. Before I can talk myself out of it, I'm downloading a less common dating app, making a profile in the hopes that Billy won't stumble across it.

But who am I kidding? At this point, I don't care if he sees it. He isn't fulfilling my needs anyway. I finish setting up my profile and start swiping immediately, barely glancing at biographies. I'm more focused on their looks, because a quick hookup will be enough to satisfy my needs.

After scrolling for about ten minutes, the matches rolling in. One guy, James, catches my eye, and I instantly type out a message: *"Hey, I'm Mariah. I am heading to the Strider Bar for a drink at noon if you want to join me."*

Seconds go by, and I am filled with anticipation. Putting myself out there could blow up in my face, but then again, it's not like my husband does anything but hang out with his buddies and play video games A notification pings, and James's reply pops up: *"See you there."*

It's been a while since I've taken a risk like this. The fact that I am married probably makes matters worse, but I need someone who can momentarily take my mind off my shitty husband. I could take the easy route and get a divorce, but that would be too expensive, so taking this route feels like the only option.

When I get to the Strider Bar, I notice a man who looks exactly like the picture on James' profile sitting at a booth, so I go over to join him. He greets me with a smile, and butterflies swarm my stomach when I realize I am really doing this.

We hang out for a while, making small talk and sharing a couple of beers. It seems to be going well; he doesn't even care that I still have my wedding band on.

At the end of our "date," he asks me if I want to go back to his place, and I am entirely on board. Once we're inside, something comes over me, and I feel like a beast in need of her prey. I give in to him instantly, getting down on my knees at his request to suck the soul out of his dick. Just when I thought he was going to return the favor, I learn he isn't really into the idea of pleasing me. Instead, he pulls out a condom and tears it open with his mouth before sheathing his large dick with it.

Instantly, he grips my legs and presses me up against the wall. He slowly pushes the head of his dick into my entrance, attempting to 'warm me up.' Assuming he'll continue with slow strokes, I'm surprised when he picks up the pace, fucking me ruthlessly against the wall. I've never been taken like this before, but to say it's good is an understatement.

We move to the bed, and little to my surprise, he pulls me on top of his face. I ride him for a few minutes while he nips and sucks at my bud before sliding me back down on his dick. His pace continues, and after about thirty minutes, I realize this is far better than anything I've received from Billy.

When we finish, we slip our clothes back on and move to the kitchen. He grabs us each a beer, and I take a few sips, still catching my breath. After I finish, he pulls out a bag of white powder. He pours some onto the counter, lines it up, and snorts it.

Never having done drugs before, I don't know what to do or think. He looks at me, grinning, and lays out a line for me. "Your turn," he says.

Fuck it. I lean down and follow his lead.

The burn hits just as instant as the regret. I know I shouldn't have done that. But what I don't know is if I can ever undo the decision I just made.

SCHOOL O
SOCIAL WO

Mariah

PRESENT DAY

A few weeks pass, and classes with Cyrus aren't as weird as I thought they'd be. We've met outside of class at a diner a few times, and I have even gone over to his apartment. I know I'm pushing boundaries, but his obsession with me is obvious, and that makes me feel like I have no choice but to cooperate.

To my surprise, he maintains a professional relationship with me in the classroom. There have been a couple of times when he's tried to kiss me in public, but I've always pulled away before anything can happen. I can tell this frustrates him, but that's one line I refuse to let him cross.

After class today, he asked if he could come over, and I agreed. Navigating him is difficult, and I always have to be careful since he holds the upper hand. He cooks us spaghetti and meatballs, cleans up without a word, and we decide to watch a scary movie. Not even five minutes in, he leans over and kisses me on the cheek.

It brings me back to the first time we were in my apartment after leaving the Strider Bar, and it sparks something in me. Turning, I kiss him, which I know I shouldn't have done, and he definitely won't leave me alone now. There is no going back.

He lays me down on the couch, kissing my neck and making his way down. Boy, have I missed this. I have my doubts, but the truth is, I need the release. And before I know it, he is lifting my dress to gain access to my aching pussy. Looking at me, his eyes flash with heat like he's ready to devour every inch of me.

Breathing deeply, he moves until his tongue glides over my clit. Shockwaves flood my body because I know he is about to please me until my legs won't stop shaking. As if reading my mind, Cyrus slowly inserts two fingers inside me, a moan tumbling from my lips. He picks up his pace in response, fucking me with his fingers while he continues to suck on my clit.

It's one of the best feelings.

Slowly, he pulls out before freeing his dick from his pants. My mouth waters at the sight; it's been a while since I felt him inside of me, and I just know he's going to fuck the shit out of me. As I contemplate if this is right or not, I ultimately give in to the desire for more.

Cyrus picks me up and carries me over to my bedroom, easing me down on my back. He hovers over me, and in one quick motion he lifts my legs up. Placing them on his shoulders, he gives me no time to adjust, slamming inside of me so far that I can feel him in my stomach. He picks up the pace, each thrust more unrelenting than the last. I moan his name, begging him to go deeper, and he instantly follows my request. I feel the orgasm building inside of me, and before I know it, I feel my release coat him and the sheets underneath us.

And still, Cyrus doesn't stop. He continues pushing into me, only to pull out and flip me onto my stomach. He reaches around my body, placing his hands around my neck and slightly squeezing. It feels amazing, and another orgasm builds inside me.

He continues choking me until stars line my vision, but he pulls away right before I would go unconscious. As soon as oxygen greets me, another orgasm rips through my body and Cyrus pulls out to shoot his cum all over my back.

Like the gentleman he was last time, he goes to the bathroom and grabs a washcloth to clean me up.

When he finishes, we put our clothes back on and head to the living room, where we pour ourselves another glass of wine. I wait for him to say something, but he doesn't. Instead, he just stares at me intensely.

"So, Cyrus..." I start, but he cuts me off.

"That was amazing, and I can't wait for us to do it again," he says, his voice filled with certainty.

I expected this, but I can't let it continue. "Cyrus, this was a mistake. It shouldn't have happened. We should be keeping things professional. I only agreed to go on these small dates with you to keep my secret safe, but sex was just not supposed to be part of it."

For a moment, it looks like he's about to respond, but instead he grabs his things in silence and walks out the front door.

I don't know how I feel about this, and what might come next now that I denied him again.

for wha
to be be
point o
Blackn
obtair
by thr
expos

CHAPTER 17

Cyrus

I don't understand why she won't give in and take all of me. Keeping this secret isn't working anymore; I need her. I feel consumed by her.

Tonight only proved it. Being with her, having sex like that, was just the icing on the cake. It made me realize how much I can't live without her. I feel like all she sees me as is her enemy, a man holding her secrets over her head, and that makes her resent me in every way.

I want her to be happy, but my happiness is just as important. And if I can't have her, then I don't know how I'll ever find it. Maybe I'm acting crazy but I know one thing: I'll do anything I can to make her mine.

When I get back to my apartment, I pull out a

piece of paper and start writing a note—something I'll slip under Mariah's office door. I don't know how she will feel when she reads it, but it's time I got things off my chest. Maybe this is a bad idea, but I no longer care.

SCHOOL O
SOCIAL WO

After doing the line James laid out for me, I feel like I've slipped into a different universe. They say drugs can take your mind off of things and transport you to another place, and that's exactly what's happening now.

James seems completely fine. Maybe that's what comes with experience, with doing this often. Maybe one day, that will be me.

I never thought a simple hookup in a bar would lead me here, but it did.

I sit on the couch in his home, spacing off. Before I know it, James is shaking me awake.

When I finally check the time, it's seven in the morning. How did I sleep this long? Looking down at my phone, I see multiple texts from Billy.

Are you okay?

Where are you?

Why aren't you answering me?

You are making me very worried.

Please pick up the phone and let me know you are okay.

I am sorry about how I have been treating you lately. I promise things will be different.

Of course, I disappear for a short amount of time, and suddenly he's promising things will be different. How am I supposed to believe that? He hasn't shown he's cared in a long time. I type out a short reply, knowing it'll probably piss him off since I don't bother answering all of his questions.

I'm fine.

I am over having to answer him and his constant demands, so I look up at James and plant a kiss on his lips. What I really need is for him to fuck me the way he did last night, to take my mind off the chaos that surrounds Billy and my relationship.

James doesn't hesitate, his mouth instantly crashing into mine. The two of us proceed to have the same mind-blowing sex as we did last night, but with some added positions thrown in. Who would have known that a man fucking me from the side could feel this good?

We go at it for about ten minutes until James is ready to hit another line. I follow his lead, realizing this might be the start of something I'm not ready for. I told myself last night's hit would be the only one, but there's something about him that's convincing, something that encourages me to let out my inner demons. Who gives a shit what Billy thinks? I am just a girl having the time of her life, and for once, it feels good.

Hours slip by, and I decide to return home to Billy so he can see that I am, in fact, okay. Maybe then he won't send a search party to look for me.

When I walk through the front door, he's on the couch, waiting. When he hears me, he jumps up and runs over, like he actually cares that I'm home. It shocks me. For months now, it's felt like we're just roommates, not a married couple.

I humor him for a moment while he tells me how much he was worried about me and wants to improve our relationship. It all sounds like BS to me, but I guess we'll see if anything changes.

I give in and admit that I didn't come home because I hooked up with someone else. I tell him it was because I felt like he wasn't delivering on his end, no matter how much I tried. What I don't tell him is about the drugs I did last night and this morning. He's furious at first, but tells me that he'll do better moving forward, that he'll give me what I need. I want to believe him. I really do because I don't want to cheat on my husband again. But I know if he doesn't do his part, it just won't work out anymore. I'll be forced to make the decision of having to leave him.

Maybe one day I'll find the courage to tell him about the drugs.

After a moment of contemplation, I head upstairs to the shower and wash away all of the things that happened last night and this morning. I turn the knob to make the water as hot as possible and begin scrubbing my skin of my infidelity.

With my eyes closed and the water running down my body, I hear the shower door open. Billy steps in, his hands running along the side of my body before his lips press against my neck. He whispers that he misses seeing me like this. For a moment, I want to laugh, but if my husband wants me, then I'll let him.

SIX MONTHS LATER

Billy and I had sex for about three weeks before everything went downhill again. When he noticed that I was fine and coming home regularly every day, he started to decrease his need for me. Sometimes, he wouldn't look at me, and other times he refused to get in bed with me. So, what did I do? I slipped back into old habits—hooking up with whoever, whenever—but I always found my way back to James. He gave me the perfect dose of whatever I needed to float on a cloud and forget about everything going on around me.

It didn't take long for the realization to hit me: I was addicted to the substances James was feeding me. Deep down, I knew I would eventually have to seek treatment if I ever wanted the chance to chase my dream of becoming a social worker.

One day, I finally told Billy about my addiction and the support I needed. He said he wished I had told him sooner because, then maybe, he could have stopped it from going this far. It was one of the hardest conversations we'd ever had, but for once, I opened up. I told him how invisible I felt in our marriage and how unheard I had been for so long.

That day, we sat together and cried. We talked about how much our marriage had gone downhill, and whether it could even survive without honesty and communication. In the end, we agreed to be there for one another and talk through the chaos, concerns, and our needs to try to make things work until they couldn't anymore.

SCHOOL O
SOCIAL WO

Sometimes I think my past catches up to me with my willingness to give in to what others want. I keep thinking about the night I had with Cyrus, knowing I should push it out of my mind, but I am having a hard time letting it go. Maybe I shouldn't have hooked up with him, but the past can't be changed now.

When I get to my office, I unlock the door and step inside. As I turn to close it, I spot an envelope addressed to me on the floor. Instantly, I bend down and grab it. Tearing it open, I find a letter written in a handwriting I know far too well.

> Mariah,
>
> I had an amazing time with you the other night, an I am so grateful that I could spend that time with you. Something about you makes me feel so absorbed in you and your life. Who would have thought a hookup on your 30th birthday would have turned us into this wonderful couple that we are today?
>
> They say sometimes, when you know, you know. That is exactly how I feel about you. I am thankful that I get to spend these days and moments with you. I can't wait to see what else is in store for us, but know that I will continue to want you each and every day.
>
> -Cyrus

"What the fuck," I mutter out loud.

This man is delusional if he thinks we are in an actual relationship. That whole "feeling invested in me" thing unsettles me. As a student, he shouldn't be consumed by me and my being. I feel like no matter what boundaries I set, he won't respect them. He sees me as his woman, and I don't think that's something I can stop.

Lately, I've been thinking about what would happen if the truth of my past—my infidelity and drug use—got out. It might damage my career, but I have been clean for a while now, and part of me believes people would see how much I have changed.

I've done the work. I went to rehab. I turned my life around. That part of my past was never public knowledge, so there are no charges against me for it. Maybe, just maybe, that will work out in my favor.

I need to stop living in fear of my past resurfacing. If there's one thing I've learned, it's that I wouldn't be here today without those mistakes. What happened back then doesn't define me now. I was dumb and reckless, but that's not who I am anymore. I need to start owning that truth instead of hiding from it.

I am clean. I haven't craved drugs since. When I look back, I see a woman desperate for an outlet, desperate to escape the grip of a marriage that made me feel powerless. Yeah, I made some bad choices back then, but I don't regret the journey life took me on.

Cyrus can't hold me back anymore. If he wants to expose my past, then so be it. Maybe I was never meant to be a teacher in the first place.

They say your past always catches up to you, and now mine finally has. I know I need to sit down and have a conversation with Cyrus, but I don't know how he'll react if I tell him to go ahead and release it. My eyes fall to the tattoo on my foot—*Never give up.* At this moment, I know it's time for me to hold my head high. Whatever Cyrus chooses to do, I'll have to accept it.

With that thought, I collect myself and head to the classroom where I know he'll be. The conversation has to happen, but not yet. Not while class is in session. This talk could change everything, and I need the strength to face it when the time comes.

for wha

to be be

point o

Blackm

obtain

by thr

expos

I watch Mariah as she walks into the classroom, her expression carrying something that looks like sadness. I wonder if she went to her office and got my letter, or if she's upset about something else. I hope I didn't say something that made her feel the way that she does right now. If I did, I regret it already. Maybe I should have considered her perspective on her resistance. All I wanted was for her to see how I feel about her.

Class goes on like usual, but at the end, Mariah asks me to stay after. It's out of the ordinary for her, something she's never done before.

I still can't bring myself to call her *Professor White*, not after I've had my dick inside of her. It just doesn't feel right to address her like that.

My mind swirls with the anticipation. Maybe

she's going to tell me that she read my letter and feels the same way. Or maybe she'll say the opposite; that she hates me and wants me out of her life. I try to quiet my thoughts, but they keep spiraling.

"Cyrus, we need to talk," she finally says.

I look at her intently, waiting for her to go on before I respond.

"I received your letter," she continues, "and I am having a hard time wrapping my head around it. You expressed how you feel invested in me and how we are the perfect couple. But, Cyrus, we're not... We aren't a couple. I am not sure of where the disconnect is, but the contents of that letter are simply not true."

Her words land, and I don't know if I should feel sad or furious. I draw in a deep breath, steadying myself before I respond.

Before I find the courage to say anything, she cuts in.

"Go ahead and release the information you found if that's what your heart desires. I can't keep living as a victim to you, doing everything you want me to. If you expose my infidelity or drug use, then you'll get the satisfaction of giving out information that nobody else knows about or should know about. But I am done living in fear. I'm done holding myself to everyone else's expectations. So if you see the need to release the information, then you do it. I won't stop you."

My jaw nearly hits the floor. That's not where I thought this conversation was going. I expected her to tell me how much she appreciated the letter, maybe even that she cared about me too. Instead, she's looking at me like I'm the enemy, and, for a moment, I'm too stunned to speak.

"Mariah, I really don't want to release this information," I finally state. Her expressions shifts, confusion and disbelief clouding it.

"I love you." I go on, the words tumbling out before I can stop them. "From the moment I saw you, I knew you were the one I'd fall for, and that's exactly what happened. I don't even know why I fell for you so quickly, but there's just something about you that I can't let go of. I don't want to ruin your career. That was never the point. I only held onto that information because I thought it would keep you close; make you fall for me too. But it doesn't seem like you will."

Her silence weighs on me, but I push forward anyway.

"My grades are slipping because I can't stop thinking about you. Every day and every moment you're all I see. I know this relationship isn't ideal, not with you being my professor, but I promise I can keep it a secret until I graduate. I want all of you, and I know deep down that you want me too."

All I can focus on is the shock on her face. Her eyes widen, then narrow, and before I know it, she's pacing back and forth across the room. My confessions hang between us, impossible to take back.

I needed to be honest with her. I've never liked to sugarcoat things because you never get anywhere by doing that. At least now she knows exactly where I stand.

SCHOOL O
SOCIAL WO

I can't believe this man just declared his love for me here, in my classroom. How can he claim to love me when we've only known each other for such a short period of time? I don't feel the same way; at least, I don't think I do. There are no butterflies when I'm around him, but maybe that isn't how those feelings are supposed to surface.

This was only supposed to be a one-night stand. Yet hooking up with him the other day seems to have convinced him that he does have deep feelings for me. And now I can't shake the thought that I might have led him on, even though I have tried to make my intentions clear the moment I realized he was my student. I never wanted to become *that* professor—the one romantically involved with a student, the kind of scandal that sometimes makes headlines. But here I am, standing in the middle of it.

I pace the room, replaying everything from the night we met at the bar to now. The same thought keeps arising: What have I done? And what do I do next?

I let out a sigh, forcing myself to slow down to gather the right words to express myself.

"Cyrus, I don't know how you love me. This was not how it was supposed to go. You weren't supposed to catch feelings for me. You need to really think about this. I can help you get your grades up, but it can't be anything more than that."

His expression shifts with my offer. I know it isn't what he wanted to hear based off the disappointment in his eyes, but this is how it *has* to be.

"I guess you can help me with my grades," he replies. "Maybe if I dive into school, I can take my mind off of everything you do to me. Maybe these feelings will fade. I think I can get back to my studies and can have a successful rest of the year."

I am shocked that he agreed so quickly, but equally relieved. I don't want to see a student fail, especially with something they're so passionate about. Still, worry still lingers in the back of my mind. The more we spend time together, the more dangerous this becomes. We can catch even more feelings when we least expect them, and I need to do my absolute best to keep that from happening.

SCHOOL O
SOCIAL WO

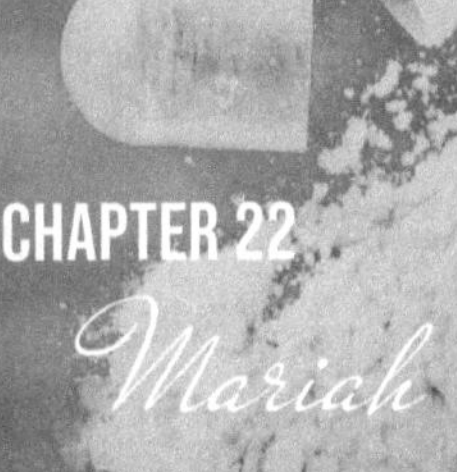

After a night of rest, I decided that my first lesson with Cyrus will take place today, in my office at the school. Remembering what it was like to get my degree, I want him set up for success. My studies had their ups and downs, but I was grateful when I walked across the stage, witnessing my hard work finally paid off.

Even if he thinks about me a lot, I want the same for him. He needs to put those thoughts aside when we are together so he can focus on the topics we are going through. It helps that I already have experience with these courses, considering I've been a student here before, so I have learned a significant amount of the material. With him not submitting his work on time, his grade isn't the highest in my class, but it's something he can improve. I have always wanted to be an accommodating professor, and because of that, I will allow him to submit late work and still give him some credit for it.

While sitting at my office desk, there's a knock at the door. I look up to see Cyrus, and I invite him in. Today, I've planned for us to review the course topics in my class to make sure he understands my expectations. He comes in, and sits in the seat directly across from my desk. Immediately, we begin our lesson, and he remains engaged, answering every question I ask. It's a good start because it shows he wants to improve.

None of the other students have swung by during my office hours but, with Cyrus here, I'm happy to finally help someone out—even if it's outside of my traditional hours. I hope that in helping him, he can move on to bigger and better things. But there is a part of me that is doubtful, knowing he still wishes to see me outside of the classroom.

A few hours pass, and Cyrus asks me if he can buy me coffee. I happily agreed. Since being clean, I've always turned to coffee. It gives me the energy I need without the risk and, as my peer recovery specialist recommended, it helped me curb my cravings.

We snag our drinks from the counter, just a few

blocks from campus. "Mariah, is there any way you can come back to my apartment so we can talk?"

We are supposed to start fresh today, but perhaps a conversation wouldn't hurt.

We get to his apartment, coffees in hand. He unlocks the door and allows me to pass before shutting it behind me, the two of us heading to the couch. Out of the countless times I've been here, there's something that feels different; more serious. It's as if he believes this conversation can change everything.

We sit down and Cyrus sighs. "Mariah, I don't want to expose your past, but I do want to learn more about what happened. Why did your ex use infidelity and drug use against you in your divorce?"

Shock floods my system. This is information I haven't shared with anyone because it's a vulnerability I don't want to be judged for. But since Cyrus has already read about what happened, I decide it is fine for me to open up about what happened.

"Well, as you know, I was married up until this school year started. Everything seemed good to everyone on the outside, but things happened behind closed doors. Billy was great initially, don't get me wrong, but he changed after we were together for a while. He wasn't as affectionate and loving as he was during our engagement. Sometimes, he wouldn't sleep in the same bed as me, and our intimacy stopped completely. Eventually, I got tired of it, downloaded a dating app, and met up with a new man—the man responsible for getting me hooked on narcotics after only one night of us being together.

"I didn't anticipate that I'd become addicted. But who really can? When I first told Billy about my drug use, it felt like he cared and wanted to support me. But that didn't last long. Without his claimed support, I went back to using. I genuinely thought I'd lose my life to it, and when my neighbor found me outside high as a kite, I knew I had to stop. Instead of turning me in, he referred me to a rehab center where I ended up getting sober. After it all, it was too late with Billy. He'd threatened divorce for so long, and I'd convinced myself he wouldn't go through with it, but he did."

Wiping a tear from my eye, I curse at myself internally. I don't know why I let all of this come out of me, but it did. Cyrus grabs my hands and goes to speak, but I cut him off before he has the chance. "I don't need you to feel bad for me, and I understand if me opening up about this makes you want to release the information even more, but I needed this release. I haven't been able to express these feelings about my past to anyone, so thank you."

This is exactly what I needed, and instead of judging me, Cyrus wipes the tears from my cheeks and kisses my forehead.

"You are strong and brave for telling me what happened." He offered a soft smile before continuing, "I'm sorry that you went through that, but I'm thankful you trusted me because I can tell you needed that release. I understand that sometimes you might think I'm crazy, but I want you to know that you can trust and confide in me. The only thing I want is to help you get through the stress of it all."

His words make me cry harder. I've never had a man care so much about me, to allow me to express myself and what I've gone through. Maybe Cyrus was right when he said we were good together. Maybe I've put up a barrier to protect my heart from getting hurt again. Maybe there is something between us.

But it's not something I can think about. This type of relationship is forbidden in the academic world, and still I can't help but wonder how things could be between us.

Knowing I need to take a breather, I only hope the feelings inside will subside with it. "Cyrus, it is getting late and it would be best for me to head home. Thank you for listening to me. I will see you in class tomorrow."

With that, I leave. Once I walk through the door, I immediately head upstairs and get in the shower. The emotions become too overwhelming for me to handle, and I begin bawling. Maybe Cyrus is the person for me, but I know this is wrong. He blackmailed me and threatened to release my past to the world. How could I ever fall for someone like that? Maybe, just maybe, I have fallen for him to a certain extent, but I can't let myself commit to those feelings.

I need to take some time to reflect on everything that's happened between us and really figure out where my feelings stand.

SCHOOL O
SOCIAL WO

CHAPTER 23

Mariah

ONE MONTH LATER

Classes have been progressing, and I've given a lot of thought to myself and my relationship with Cyrus. The time allowed me to come to terms that I've felt something for him all along, but I just couldn't own up to it.

Ever since we sat down, we've met twice a week to review social work topics, and his grades have improved substantially. He hasn't brought up releasing the information of my past, and after the night we talked, I think he finally understood me. I am still grateful I was able to experience that release; it was like a weight was finally lifted from my chest.

Over the last few weeks, we have alternated between meeting in my office, my apartment, and his apartment. We haven't hooked up since the last time we were together, but we have continued to have deep conversations that have brought us closer. Cyrus told me more about his past, a time where he was homeless, and a time that shaped his desire to become a social worker. Inspired, I told him about my path to becoming a teacher and how it wasn't always easy. Each conversation brought us closer, and I'm afraid I'm starting to fall for him the same way he has for me, he doesn't know it yet.

I went so long blocking out the possibility of developing feelings for him, but I think I've finally come to realize the chemistry between us. He is so easy to talk to, and sometimes, I catch myself over-looking the fact that he is still my student. We keep everything professional in the classroom, but as soon as we leave, the laughter we share is unmatched. We've grown to know one another so well, and I know I can't confess my feelings to him. Not yet. Not when I've been hurt as bad as I have in the past.

All I've ever wanted was for him to be successful. He has been interning at a homeless shelter and tells me about it all the time. I can tell he's starting to reach his goals, and he truly seems happy in doing so. This is what brings me joy as a professor; to see him excelling in what he wants.

I am genuinely happy we've got to this point.

Finally deciding it's time to tell him how I feel, I can't help but feel anxious. So instead, I write a letter that I plan to give to him the next time I see him.

Cyrus,

Thank you for all the joy you have made me feel over this past month. You have truly made me feel special and wanted. I have always been able to open up to you, so I am truly thankful for that. I want you to know that, as hard as I have been trying to avoid this feeling, I am falling for you.

There is something about you that brings me joy. Thinking that I would have considered you my enemy not too long ago is crazy to think about. Today, I want to consider you my lover and not let anything get in between that.

With the roles we are in right now, we would need to keep it a secret for a while, but in the end, it will all be worth it. If you're down for this, then I am too.

With love,
M

I TAKE THE LETTER, CHOOSING TO SLIDE IT UNDER HIS apartment door on my way home, unable to wait any longer. Even though I'm nervous about how he'll respond, I know that I need to express my feelings for him. Writing it on paper is so much easier because I don't have to humiliate myself by talking to him face-to-face, especially after all the times I rejected him.

I know he feels the same, but I'm not sure if he'll be okay with keeping everything a secret until he graduates. At this point, it's a waiting game.

for wha
to be be
point o
Blackr
obtain
by thr
expos

CHAPTER 24

Cyrus

After going out a couple days this week with Sean and Mariah, I decided to pick up a shift. I can't stop thinking about the past month. Mariah and I are getting closer, but part of me wonders if I'm going crazy over my desire for us to get together. Maybe she does not see us in the same way as I do, and I would hate to bring up how I feel again after all the problems it's caused.

Lunch hour comes to an end, and the restaurant slows down, my boss cutting me loose early. Before leaving, I complete my end-of-shift tasks: rolling silverware and napkins. Once I finish, I head back to my apartment.

After turning the key, I nudge my door open, spotting a note addressed to me on the floor. Snatching it, I make my way to my room and place it on my bed so I can hop in the shower. Typically, this is how it goes because I don't have the desire for my whole apartment to smell like seafood. It takes two rounds of me scrubbing my hair and body for me to remove the scent.

Once I finish, I wrap a towel around my waist, heading back to open the letter. Opening it, I immediately spot Mariah's familiar handwriting, reading the contents entirely. It contains a confession of Mariah's feelings for me, a moment I've been waiting for for months.

I instantly pull out my phone and shoot her a quick text.

> We need to talk. I will swing by your apartment in ten minutes.

Not even five seconds later, she replies.

> Come in when you get here; the door is unlocked.

Part of me is furious that Mariah left her door unlocked. There are too many creeps out there, and the idea of one of them getting in irritates me beyond measure. But maybe she doesn't usually leave it unlocked, and she is just doing it for me.

One can hope.

I quickly get ready, rushing out the front door. In

a matter of minutes, I get to her apartment and let myself in, which is a strange feeling. I'm not used to letting myself in, so walking in on my own accord is out of the ordinary.

Once inside, I spot Mariah sitting on the kitchen counter. She scrolls on her phone with a glass of red wine in her hand. As the door clicks shut behind me, she puts it down. I can't help but run to her, and once my arms are around her, my lips meet hers.

Before getting lost in our kiss, she pulls back. "I guess you got my letter then." She laughs before continuing, "I'm sorry for putting this off for so long. I wanted to hate you for holding that information over my head, but you showed me that you aren't the person I thought you were. When I actually sat down and talked to you, I realized there was so much more about you that I didn't know. When I started to fall for you, my stupidity took over, and I swallowed my feelings. I really hope you understand why I went about things this way."

Cutting her off, my lips crashed into hers. In between each kiss, I tell her I love her, and she says it back. There's nothing that feels better than to hear those words come out of her mouth.

Picking her up, I take her to her bedroom and we make sweet love. It's different from what we've done in the past, but I take my time exploring every inch of her body.

When we finish, we lie together. Neither of us say a word as we stare into each other's eyes, but after a few minutes, I break the silence. "I am perfectly fine being your little secret. But the moment I graduate, you best believe the world will know you're mine."

She smiles and kisses me, pulling back to say, "Thank you for being my outlet. I will love you today, tomorrow, and for as long as possible. Even though the professional world forbids our relation-ship, I won't let anything come between us. You will continue finishing the rest of your studies and, come next year, once you graduate, we can be together in front of the world."

With her dedication, I kiss her. We continue to lie together until she drifts into a deep slumber, and I cradle her against me, basking in the moment.

Who would have thought enemies could become lovers in the end?

SCHOOL O
SOCIAL WO

This past year with Cyrus has been amazing. We've learned to keep our relationship from other's eyes, and he's continued to come to my apartment to stay the night since he has a roommate. Throughout it all, we've only grew as a couple, and he's finally reached the point of graduation.

I am so proud of him, and happy that he gets to live his dream of being a social worker. I've seen him in action at the homeless shelter where he completed his internship, and I've witnessed how he values the dignity and worth of every person he interacts with. He upholds the social work principles and values, and I can't wait to see him cross the stage. He deserves the degree he's been working for these past few years.

Our love has grown significantly, and we've

discussed the idea of moving in together. We decided that, once he's officially graduated, he'll move into my apartment, and we'll start our lives together.

Who would have thought I'd fall for someone younger than me? Someone off-limits? I know I sure as hell didn't, but I don't regret it happening.

When I wake up, Cyrus remains curled up beside me. Nudging him, I tell him that it's time for him to get ready for graduation. He hates it when I wake him up, but I can't let him sleep through his big day. Getting ready for the ceremony together, I can't help but admire him. Once he finishes, he kisses me on the forehead.

"I will see you later," he says, heading for the front door. "I love you."

"I love you, too," I reply as I finish my coffee. Once I triple check I have everything I need, I head out for the ceremony.

The graduation program flies by. Maybe it's because I've sat here anxiously, awaiting the reveal of our relationship once he receives his diploma.

When it ends, he kisses me in front of everyone. My heart drums in my chest because I don't know what anyone else will see but, when I pull away, I'm greeted with smiles. It's as if everyone was aware of what was going on between us.

Before I congratulate him, he gets down on one knee. Opening the box, a beautiful ring glistens in the sunlight filtering in through the windows. Immediately, I tear up. We'd only briefly discussed marriage, so his decision to propose completely caught me off guard.

After my divorce, I'd always hesitated to get married again. But this is different. I *know* it will work out. Our communication is solid, and our ability to express what bothers us has only grown; both of which are key to any relationship.

"Mariah, I have loved you since the moment I saw you at Strider Bar. Some people don't believe in love at first sight, but I do. I experienced it when I met you. And while you tried to push me away because of your fear of getting hurt, I'm glad you let me in. I want to spend forever with you because you are perfect, and I can't see myself with anyone else."

Everyone around us waits for a response. The words are stuck in my throat, but as soon as Cyrus' eyes meet mine, they come out easily. "Of course, I will marry you!"

It was the best 'yes' I've said in a long time, and I can't wait to see where this life with Cyrus takes me. I know I've put off our relationship for a while, and that it may seem rushed to others, but I truly don't care what anyone else thinks. I've found the man who makes me feel good about myself, a man who has helped support me when the thoughts of my past threatened to consume me.

And for that, I am grateful for him and hopeful for our future.

SCHOOL O
SOCIAL WO

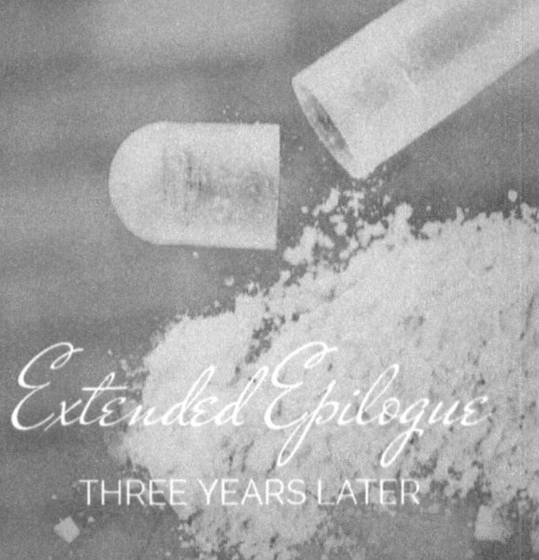

Extended Epilogue

THREE YEARS LATER

Three years have passed, and I never would have imagined being in the position I am now. Cyrus has been excellent to me ever since he graduated. He has been able to carry out his dreams of working in a homeless shelter. The stories he tells me when he gets off from work sometimes break my heart because these families have gone through some unimaginable things.

While Cyrus is excelling in his career, I have been able to continue to teach social work courses. Being able to help students find their passion in the social work field has been rewarding. I have connected students with different community organizations to help them get firsthand experience in areas where they would like to work in the future. That is one of my favorite parts about being a professor. I hope that in the future, students will remember me and how I helped them grow not only as students but also as social work professionals.

I have done so much reflecting over the past few years about everything I have overcome. I journal regularly to help put my feelings down about who I used to be and who I am now. When thinking about my past of being addicted to drugs and not doing right by my ex-husband, it makes me think of how I should have done things differently. I should have broken it off sooner and not put him through the pain he faced.

My past doesn't define who I am today, but it has influenced me to become a better person, especially when it comes to Cyrus. Initially, I wasn't sure how things would go between us, but when he asked me to marry him on graduation day, I knew he would be my forever person. I knew I wanted things to be different in this relationship than with Billy, so

I opted to go into individual and couples counseling. This has allowed me to cope with my past and learn how to become a better partner.

Cyrus and I decided we didn't want to wait too long to get married after he proposed. Wedding planning was a little stressful at first because we didn't know who we should invite and didn't want to spend much money. We opted to have a fifty-person wedding surrounded by our family and closest friends. It was lovely. We did an outdoor wedding with sunflowers as our theme. The vows that Cyrus read made me cry even though I tried to be strong and hold back my tears. He knows how to make a woman feel special.

We went back and forth on whether we wanted to do a honeymoon but ultimately decided to go to Grand Turk for a few days. The island was amazing, and the water was so blue. We went on an island tour and tried the local beer. It was such a great experience until I learned that maybe I shouldn't have been drinking on the honeymoon.

When Cyrus and I returned from Grand Turk, my body didn't feel right. I had been throwing up and was very tired all the time. I decided to go to the local pharmacy and grabbed a pregnancy test to take. I went back and forth on if I should wait for Cyrus to get home from work, but the anticipation was killing me, so I said fuck it and took it. Within a matter of seconds, the word "pregnant" appeared on the screen, causing me to bawl my eyes out.

Fear filled me because I wasn't sure how I could be a mother with how my past went. What if I wasn't the mother my child needed me to be? These negative thoughts started to overtake me, but I knew that if I put my mind to being the best mother I could be, then I would be. With Cyrus coming home within the next few hours, I knew I needed to find a way to tell him I was pregnant, so I ran to the store to pick up a onesie and a box to put the positive test result and onesie in.

When Cyrus got him from work, I asked him to sit down and open the box. As soon as he pulled the lid off, tears began to fill his eyes. I couldn't tell if they were happy or sad tears until he stood up and wrapped me in the biggest hug. After our initial emotions started to go away, we decided to sit down and have a talk about the pregnancy and what we should do. I expressed my reservations about being a mother, and he supported me throughout the conversation. Ultimately, we decided that we wanted to have the baby.

The next morning, I contacted my OBGYN, who was able to get me in because they had a cancellation. When we got to our appointment, we had a blood test that showed I was indeed pregnant, and we got scheduled for an ultrasound at the end of the week. We could see our baby at the ultrasound appointment and hear the heartbeat. Dr. James said I was eight weeks pregnant, which caught me entirely off guard. Apparently, some people can go a while being pregnant without even knowing. Luckily, the baby was completely healthy.

A few months later, we discovered we were having a baby girl. We instantly started ordering items for our nursery and landed on the name Lillian Rose for her. Preparing for the arrival of our baby girl was fun but stressful at the same time. I continued getting individual therapy to help cope with becoming a new mother, and as time went on, I truly believed I could be a great mother with the help of Cyrus. Every night, he would kiss my stomach and talk to Lillian so she could hear his voice. Seeing this made me fall more and more in love with him.

The day Lillian Rose was born, she weighed 7.5 pounds and was 20 inches long. Everyone calls her Cyrus's mini-me because they look so much alike. Seeing how Cyrus holds and cares for her brings me so much joy. I love every part of them both and can't wait to see what our future holds from here on out.

Acknowledgments

Thank you all for reading my debut book. I was nervous about writing it, but I am glad I pushed forward and did it. This is a revamped version of it, so I hope you all enjoy these characters the same.

I would like to thank my PA Stephanie for always supporting me and pushing me to continue writing!

Thank you to my street team for helping me push my books out so people can know who I am and what I write.!

Thank you to Sophie for making my vision of this book come to life with this new cover that fits the story so much more!

Deann Soleil 🌻

Deann Soleil is a self-published author based in Virginia who focuses on writing forbidden romances. When not writing, she is a full-time social worker who works with victims of community violence to help them overcome their traumatic experiences. If you're looking for short, fast-paced books, then look no further.

Chasing the Forbidden Desire

Stalked Through the Night

Tangled Up With Santa

———

Anthologies:

A Wild Run Anthology (The Chase)

Monsters, Masks & Mayhem Anthology (The Graveyard)

Love, Lust & Chestnuts Anthology (A Holiday Getaway)

Christmas Temptation Anthology (One Stop at Love)